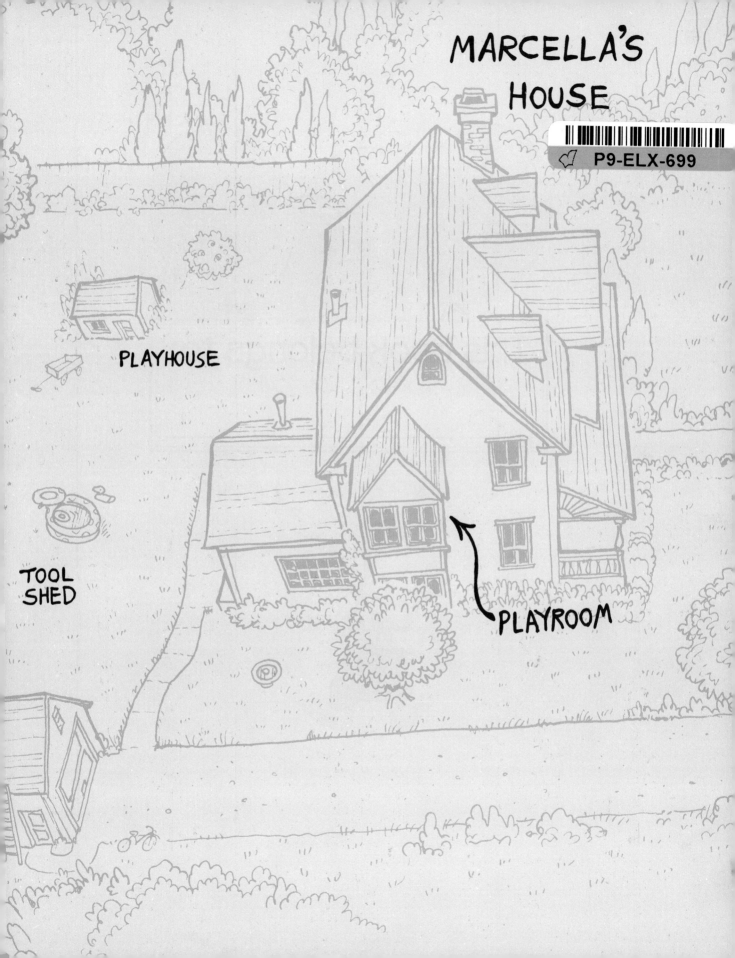

MARCELLA'S
HOUSE

PLAYHOUSE

TOOL
SHED

PLAYROOM

This book belongs to:

_____

Raggedy Ann & Andy's

GROW
AND
LEARN
LIBRARY

VOLUME 7

A VERY CLOSE CALL

A LYNX BOOK

This book is published by Lynx Books, a division of Lynx Communications, Inc., 41 Madison Avenue, New York, New York 10010. The name "Lynx" together with the logotype consisting of a stylized head of a lynx is a trademark of Lynx Communications, Inc.

Raggedy Ann and Andy's Grow-and-Learn Library, the names and depictions of Raggedy Ann, Raggedy Andy and all related characters are trademarks of Macmillan, Inc.

The dolls in Marcella's playroom had been looking forward to this day. Marcella and her parents had gone to visit Marcella's grandmother, so the dolls could play anywhere in the house they wanted.

"What should we do today?" asked The Camel with the Wrinkled Knees.

"How about a game of hide-and-seek?" answered Bubbles the Clown.

"Great idea!" said Raggedy Andy.

"We can use the whole house," added Raggedy Ann. "We'll never run out of places to hide!"

All the dolls scrambled down the stairs.
"I'll be 'It,' " said Raggedy Ann. "I'll cover my eyes
and count to ten while you go hide."
They all scattered in different directions.

Bubbles zipped off to the kitchen. The door to the pantry was open.

"The perfect hiding place!" he said to himself, ducking inside.

As he searched for something to hide behind, a gust of wind blew the door shut.

"I'll bet they'll never find me now," giggled Bubbles. "I'm going to win this game for sure!" he thought happily. Bubbles sat down on the floor among soup cans and cereal boxes and waited to see if Raggedy Ann would find him.

" . . . eight, nine, ten," called Raggedy Ann. "Ready or not, here I come!"

Raggedy Ann started looking for the other dolls. It wasn't long before she spotted something floppy among the handles sticking out of the umbrella stand.

"There you are, Sunny Bunny," cried Raggedy Ann.
"How did you ever find me?" he asked.
"Your ears gave you away," chuckled Raggedy Ann.
"But that's okay. Now you can help me find the others."

Raggedy Ann and Sunny Bunny wandered into the living room together. Raggedy Ann looked under the end tables and behind the piano.

Sunny Bunny peered into the fireplace and searched behind the big easy chair, but there was no sign of anybody.

Raggedy Ann climbed onto the sofa and leaned back against the soft cushions to think.

All of a sudden she heard a noise.

"Hey!" cried The Camel with the Wrinkled Knees, poking his head out from behind the pillows. "You found me!"

"I guess I did," said Raggedy Ann. "I hope I didn't squish you!" she said, giving him a gentle hug.

"Nah," said The Camel. "You can't squish me. What's another wrinkle or two?"

Raggedy Ann, Sunny Bunny, and The Camel with the Wrinkled Knees went off to find the other players. They tiptoed past the big grandfather clock.

"Ssshh!" whispered Sunny Bunny. "Maybe we'll take someone by surprise."

At that moment, the clock struck four.

"*Bong! Bong! Bong! Bong!*" went the chimes, and out popped Raggedy Andy from behind the clock.

"I wasn't expecting that!" cried Raggedy Andy with his hands over his ears.

"We didn't expect you either!" gasped Sunny Bunny, looking surprised.

"Now that we've found you, you can help us," said The Camel.

"It's three down and seven to go," added Raggedy Andy.

They found Tim the Toy Soldier in back of the big dictionary on the bookshelf.

Greta the Dutch Doll was behind
a flowerpot full of tulips.

And Raggedy Cat was all curled up
in a basket of yarn.

"Three guesses where Babette is hiding," said Raggedy
Andy.

They looked at each other, and then they all rushed up
the stairs.

Babette the French Doll was having such a good time
playing at Marcella's mother's dressing table that she almost
forgot about the game.

She was giving her curls a final comb when she heard
soft little footsteps and muffled giggles coming toward the
bedroom.

"Oh, my! I'd better hide," she said to herself.

She quickly jumped off the stool and scurried under the table.

"I know you're under there, Babette," laughed Raggedy Andy.

They could see the table skirt still moving.

Babette crawled out.

"Did I win?" she asked.

"No," said Raggedy Ann. "We've still got three more to go."

When they got to the kitchen, they found Raggedy
Dog sound asleep in a basket of clean clothes. As they
shook him awake, they heard a strange noise coming from
the cabinet underneath the sink.

"*Achoo! Achoo!*"

Greta opened the cabinet door and there sat Percy the Policeman Doll, sneezing up a storm.

"It's dusty in here," he sniffled. "Otherwise you never would have found me! Who's left?" he asked.

"Just Bubbles," replied Raggedy Ann.

"Where could Bubbles be?" asked Percy.

"We've been all over the rest of the house," said Raggedy Ann. "He must be here in the kitchen."

"We'd better find him soon. Marcella will be coming home with her mother and father any time now," said The Camel with the Wrinkled Knees.

"Bubbles, Bubbles!" called Andy. "Come out. Come
out wherever you are. You've won the game!"
That's just what Bubbles was waiting to hear.
"I'm in here, guys," he called.

"Where?" cried Raggedy Ann.
"In the pantry," answered Bubbles.
"Come on out, then," coaxed The Camel with the Wrinkled Knees. "It's getting late."

"I would if I could, but I can't," said Bubbles good-naturedly. "The wind blew the door shut, and I can't get it open."

"Oh, no!" cried The Camel. "What will we do?"

"I've got an idea," said Percy. "While I was hiding underneath the sink I saw some string. I can lasso the doorknob with it and pull it open."

"That will never work," said The Camel with the Wrinkled Knees, who was growing more worried by the minute.

"How will we know if we don't try?" asked Raggedy
Ann. "Go ahead, Percy. Give it a try."

Percy made a loop at the end of the string and twirled
it over his head to gain speed. Then, with a flick of his
wrist, he sent it flying toward the doorknob.

"Got it!" he cried. "Now help me pull."

Raggedy Ann and the others grabbed onto the string and pulled.

But it was no use. The door didn't budge.

"I knew it wouldn't work," said The Camel, shaking his head sadly.

"How are you doing out there?" called Bubbles.

"No luck," answered Tim. "The problem is we have to *turn* the doorknob or it won't open."

"We have to reach it first," said Percy.

"Don't worry. We'll think of something," said Raggedy Ann.

"How about moving this chair?" asked Greta.

"It looks pretty heavy," said The Camel doubtfully.

"Let's just try," suggested Raggedy Andy.

They pushed and pulled, but no matter how hard they tried, the chair wouldn't move.

"This chair is much heavier than the little playroom chairs," said Tim.

"I knew it," said The Camel sadly.

Suddenly they heard the clock strike five.

"We better think of something fast," said Raggedy Andy.

"It's no use," said The Camel.

"We can't give up," said Raggedy Ann.

"I've got it!" said Raggedy Andy. "Help me move that broom in the corner there. Then I'll climb up the broom and turn the knob."

"That will never work. You'll never make it," said The Camel with the Wrinkled Knees.

"We've got to try something," called Bubbles.

"Of course we do," said Raggedy Ann, helping the others drag the broom across the floor.

They huffed and puffed as they tried to stand it up against the wall.

When the broom was in place, Raggedy Andy wrapped his arms and legs around the handle and started to inch his way up.

"You can do it," called Tim.
"You're almost there!" shouted Greta.

"Okay," said Raggedy Andy when he reached the top. "You grab the string, and when I turn the knob, pull as hard as you can."

Raggedy Andy reached over, and without losing his balance, he placed his hands on the doorknob.

All the dolls held their breath, frightened that Raggedy Andy would fall.

Finally, Raggedy Andy turned the knob. There was a click.

"Now!" he shouted.

They pulled the string, the door opened, and out walked Bubbles with a big smile on his face.

"What took you so long?" he joked.

Then he helped everyone put the broom and string back in their places.

"I knew you could do it all along," said Bubbles.

"Well, I sure didn't," said The Camel. "I was ready to give up."

Just then they heard a car pull into the driveway. They all hurried out of the kitchen, up the stairs, and into the playroom. They found their places just in the nick of time.

"Whew! What a close call!" whispered The Camel.
"That's right," said Raggedy Ann with a big smile.
"That's why it's important that we never gave up. Always do
your best and never stop trying!"

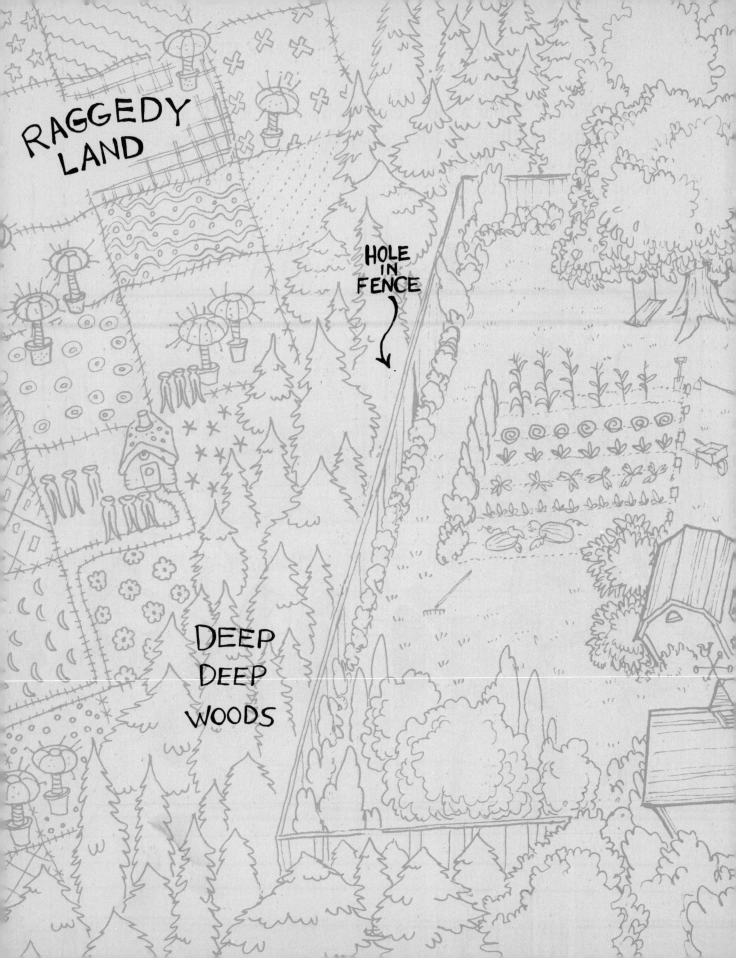